"WE SHALL NOT CEASE FROM EXPLORATION, AND THE END OF ALL OUR EXPLORING WILL BE TO ARRIVE WHERE WE STARTED AND KNOW THE PLACE FOR THE FIRST TIME."

T. S. Eliot

TO MY HAIRY
UNCIVILISED FRIEND ERIN,
WITH LOVE.

First published 2016 by Nosy Crow Ltd
The Crow's Nest, 10a Lant Street
London SE1 1QR
www.nosycrow.com

ISBN 978 0 85763 623 2 (HB)
ISBN 978 0 85763 624 9 (PB)

Nosy Crow and associated logos are trademarks
and/or registered trademarks of Nosy Crow Ltd.

Text and illustration © Frann Preston-Gannon 2016

The right of Frann Preston-Gannon to be identified as the author
and illustrator of this work has been asserted.

Printed in China by Imago
Papers used by Nosy Crow are made from wood grown in sustainable forests.

1 3 5 7 9 8 6 4 2 (HB)
1 3 5 7 9 8 6 4 2 (PB)

DAVE'S CAVE

FRANN PRESTON-GANNON

This Dave.

This Dave's cave.

Dave like cave.
Nice green grass.

Dave's friends
like cave, too.

But Dave **not** happy.
Dave wide awake.

Maybe Dave find **better**
cave with **greener** grass
and **bigger** rocks.

Dave want **new** cave.

Dave put out fire.

Off Dave go.

But first cave not **quite** right.

Second cave
not **cosy** like home.

Third cave
too noisy.

Fourth cave nice
but Dave not like pets.

Fifth cave **nice**, too . . .

HOME
SWEET
HOME

. . .. but Jon **not** like sharing.

Dave sad.

Maybe . . .

. . . no better cave,
with greener grass
and bigger rocks.

But look! This cave **nice.**

Green grass.

Big rocks.

This
cave
perfect.

This cave . . .

. . . home.